Louise Leblanc

That's Enough Maddie

Illustrations
by Marie-Louise Gay

Translated
by Sarah Cummins

Formac Publishing Company Limited
Halifax, Nova Scotia
1991

Originally published as Ça suffit, Sophie!
Copyright © 1990 la courte échelle

Translation copyright © 1991 by Formac Publishing Company
Limited

First publication in the United States 1999

Canadian Cataloguing in Publication Data

Leblanc, Louise, 1942-

[Ça suffit, Sophie. English]

That's enough, Maddie

(First novel series)

For children aged 7-10

Translation of: Ça suffit, Sophie!

ISBN 0-88780-090-04 (pbk.) — ISBN 0-88780-091-2
(bound)

I.Marie-Louise Gay. II.Title. III Title: Ça suffit, Sophie!
English IV. Series
PS8573.E25C313 1991   jC843'.54   C91-097683-X
PZ7.L43Th 1991

Formac Publishing
Limited
5502 Atlantic Street
Halifax, NS B3H 1G4

Distributed in the U.S. by:
Orca Book Publishers
P.O. Box 468 Custer, WA
U.S.A. 98240-0468

Printed and bound in Canada

Table of contents

1
Enough is enough

"Maddie, that's enough!" That's all everyone in this whole house ever says.

Do you know how many people live in this house? Six. Two parents and four kids. What a crowd! Can you believe it?

When we're all walking down the street we look like a field trip from school, with the kids following the teachers in a line. It's really embarrassing.

But the worst thing of all is that I'm the oldest. The sensible, responsible older sister who should set an example to her siblings.

There's Alexander who's seven years old and an awful grouch. And Julian who is five and wears glasses. He has only to say "You flunking bannister!" to make everyone laugh.

Then there's Angelbaby Sugarkins. She's a girl. She's two years old and supposedly adorable. Everybody's always kissing her.

As for the grown-ups in this family, they're something else.

My father is obsessed with neatness and proper English. He thinks he's always right. My mother is obsessed with cleanliness and a proper diet. She never stops moving.

When she talks, the sentences go flying over my head at the

speed of a jumbo jet. Sometimes a few words fall out like suitcases from the luggage compartment and crash onto my head.

It's usually: "Maddie, that's enough!"

Enough cookies, enough mess, enough television. Enough this, enough that.

Oh, there are a few other words that occasionally land on me. Words like "go up" and "come down."

"Come down and look after Angelbaby."

"Go up and pick up the things you left lying around."

"Come down from that tree."

"Go up to bed now."

Well, it's eight o'clock. It won't be long before I hear that last one.

"Maddie, go up to bed now. That's enough television."

What did I tell you? And that's not the worst of it.

The other day, I was with my best friend. We were talking about important things and not making any trouble. Then the three babies came in.

Two minutes later, Alexander and Julian were yelling at each other and Angelbaby was crying.

My dad came in and in his sternest voice said: "That's enough, Maddie!"

It was TOTALLY unfair!

I was so angry and embarrassed that I turned red as a tomato. And a voice inside me said, " Yes, that's enough. I have had enough! "

So I decided to leave. I can't

take it any more. I'm only nine years old. I'm too young to be the oldest!

2
Alert and awake

You need a good plan if you're going to run away from home, and I have one. I've thought of everything.

The only thing I forgot is that I will have to stay awake very late, until my parents go to bed. Right now I can hear the television. They must be watching the news. The washing machine is rumbling as it agitates the dirty laundry. Believe me, I know how that laundry feels.

Now our granny clock is striking the hour. It's my grand-mother's grandfather clock.

That's why we call it the granny clock. Sometimes it skips a stroke or two. Maybe it runs out of breath or gets forgetful, just like Gran.

No matter. If I need to know what time it is, I can check my watch.

It's ten o'clock now. I had better keep talking if I don't want to fall asleep.

Good thing that Mickey is here. I have a Mickey Mouse night-light glowing softly at the foot of my bed.

If I wake up in the middle of the night, Mickey chases away my nightmares and brings me safely back to my own room.

I like my room. The best thing about it is that I have it all to myself. At night, that is. During the

day it's more like a corner store.

They all come in and rummage through my things. Alexander even takes my dolls, but I don't care.

Julian likes to try to frighten me. He hides under my covers and then leaps up shrieking. His glasses always fall off, so I know he's not a ghost. It never scares me.

Not much can scare me. You have to be pretty brave to run away from home.

Aha! I can hear the stairs creaking. My parents are finally going up to bed. Now I have to pretend to be asleep.

Phew! They've passed my room without noticing that I have not gone sleepy-bye. That's what they tell me every night:

"Time to go sleepy-bye." Can you believe that they still say that to me, their oldest daughter who is nine years old?

If they only knew. Tonight I am not going to go sleepy-bye at all.

Still, before I go downstairs, I have to pretend to be asleep a little bit longer...just a bit... long...er....

3
Packing provisions

At last! The house is still. Everyone is asleep. The only sound is Alexander grinding his teeth. That kid's a grouch even in his sleep.

I must not make any noise as I creep downstairs. I hold my breath and try to step lightly.

It's no use. Every step I take makes the stairs creak and squeak.

I never noticed they creaked so much. But when all around there's nothing but silence, the noise they make is amazing.

Finally I reach the living room

rug, so soft and cosy. Gosh, it's dark in here!

BRRR! The kitchen tiles are freezing. They feel like icy spring water on the bottom of my feet. It's even darker in here.

I don't dare turn on the light. My parents sleep with one eye open, and they don't miss a thing.

I'll open the blinds. There! The moon is out, shining brightly. It's better than a flashlight. Oops, a flashlight — something else I didn't think of.

Fortunately, there's enough light to see by. I can fill my schoolbag with supplies. Now, what should I take?

A PROPER DIET!

Yikes, I can almost hear my mother behind me. But there's

really no one there. I still feel uneasy, though. I had better make up my mind.

Granola bars, whole-wheat bread, a box of raisins. A banana and two apples.

That's not too much. After all, I don't know what will happen to me. It might not even be enough. I have to be prepared for anything.

I fill up two sandwich bags, one with chocolate chip cookies and the other with ruffle potato chips.

I stuff a few chips in my mouth. My heart is thumping like a rock song: BABALOO BONG BONG BONG.

Along with the CRUNCH, CRUNCH, CRUNCH of the potato chips, it makes quite

a racket.

This is the first time I've been all alone in the house in the middle of the night with everyone else asleep. I never realized it would be so nerve-racking.

I am so rattled that I almost forget about the sugar-cubes, the most important item in my plan.

But I can't find the tiniest crumb of a single sugar-cube! Oh well, I guess I'll have to take this bag of brown sugar instead.

Quick, I've got to get back upstairs! Abandoning caution, I race like the wind up the stairs. CREAK, CREAK, CREAK!

I throw my school bag on the bed. CRUNCH, CRUNCH!

I burrow under the covers. PHEW!

4
A miserable life

Opening my eyes, I spy my schoolbag, about to burst its seams. Then I remember that today I have to run away from home.

My heart starts thumping out a rock song again, with a heavy drum beat. I will ignore it. I have to run away. My life is too miserable here.

Anyway, I have a very good plan and all I have to do is follow it. That's all there is to it.

Then I will be a heroine, and everyone will be sorry I'm gone.

First, I have to dress warmly:

two T-shirts, three sweaters, and my coat.

Gran often says, "In this crazy country of ours the temperature can go up and down like a yo-yo."

Then I go out to wait for the school bus. The sky is covered with clouds. Not a very reassuring sight. Brrr!

Perhaps today is not the ideal day to run away from home. Maybe my mother will stop me.

I know she'll come looking for me, because I didn't go in with the others for breakfast. When she comes, she'll notice that …

"Slept in again, did you, Maddie? Here, have this apple. You have to eat something for breakfast."

My mother came out and she

didn't notice anything amiss. Golly, we both look both pretty fat, my bag and I.

I can't believe she didn't notice a thing. I am furious at my mother, who is blind as a bat and has nothing to give me but advice. And an apple! If she knew what I have in my bag! Here's what I think of her old apple! I throw it as hard as I can.

Just my luck. At that very instant the school bus pulls up and the apple splats against the windshield right in front of Gloria.

Gloria is the bus driver. She has long red corkscrew curls that look like the wires in a toaster, and big soft eyes like a doe.

Her eyes are very big and round right now because of the apple surprise.

A bit sheepishly, I climb into the empty school bus. There's no one else there because I get picked up first on the route.

To bolster my courage I keep telling myself that I am a heroine. At the second stop I carry out the next step in my plan, by throwing my schoolbag

out the window.

"Hey, my bag fell out the window!"

Once I'm outside, I pour the brown sugar into the gas tank.

That's what crooks do so the cars won't start. I saw it in a movie once.

Actually, in the movie they used sugar-cubes. But brown sugar should work just as well, because brown sugar is much better.

5
On the main road

The school bus tootles on just as if it hadn't swallowed a thing. All the children in the neighbourhood have been picked up, and the bus hasn't broken down yet.

Gloria has turned on to the main road now. We're getting farther and farther away from home.

My plan has failed. That brown sugar is no good. Too bad! Next time I'll use sugar-cubes.

Yikes! I spoke too soon. Suddenly we're all being tossed around like popcorn in a popper.

Gloria's toaster wires fly up in the air.

Giving off a cloud of smoke, the school bus hiccups and shivers. Boing-oing-oing! POW! Huff huff huff...sproot.

One last belch, and it's over. The toaster wires settle back down.

I sigh lustily, like a heroine who must now take action.

I have planned this moment well. I know exactly what to say to create panic in a crowd.

I dash to the front of the bus, yelling "Fire! We're sinking! Help, help! Women and children first!"

It works. Panic! All the kids run after me, jostling to get off the bus.

Gloria slumps in the driver's

seat in a stupor. I've never seen
her eyes look so big.

Outside, I sneak away under
the billows of smoke.

I'm running, running. Faster

than any of the sprinters at the Olympics.

My heart is beating in time with my feet. My mouth is dry and my eyes are streaming. Before long I run out of breath. My lungs feel like they're full of brown sugar.

I stop. My face is burning and I'm dripping with sweat. After all, I do have on three sweaters and a coat. I must look like an

onion with all those layers. A big, fat, panting, red onion. If that's what I look like, everybody must be staring at me. I glance around. There's nobody there.

Just cars whizzing by. ZOOM ZOOM ZOOM.

I can't even see the school bus any more.

This time it's no joke. In my head and in the pit of my stomach, I feel real, genuine, horrible panic.

6
Keep walking, Maddie

Walk. All I can do is walk. So I walk. Down the main road. Only I don't think I'm getting anywhere. It's awful.

If only there were some houses, I could ring the doorbell. Maybe I could find some Block Parents. They're easy to spot because they have a red and white sign in the front window, with a picture of a grown-up holding a child's hand.

Maybe I could find Gran's house. She would be delighted to see me. She would spoil me rotten.

GRANNY! I should have called Gran before I made my plan. It would have been so simple.

In a tearful voice I could have

told her how unhappy I was. Gran would have said, "My poor little pumpkin, are they bothering you? Tell Granny all about it."

It would be so nice to be someone's little pumpkin again! That's the best cure for a poor martyred big sister!

Grrrr! What an idiot I am! If I had thought of calling Gran, I wouldn't be in this pickle now. I wouldn't have to keep walking for hours and hours.

The road stretches in front of me like a giant rubber band. I might be walking here for days and days.

7
Saved!

A bottle tossed by the waves in the middle of the ocean, that's what I feel like.

A bottle with a headache and sore feet.

So this is what it's like to be a heroine. Let me tell you, it's no fun. It's not a bit like the stories you hear.

In books and movies the heroines are always perky and cheerful. I am very, very tired. Any more tired than this, and I would die.

Any more downhearted than this, and I would cry. Already my

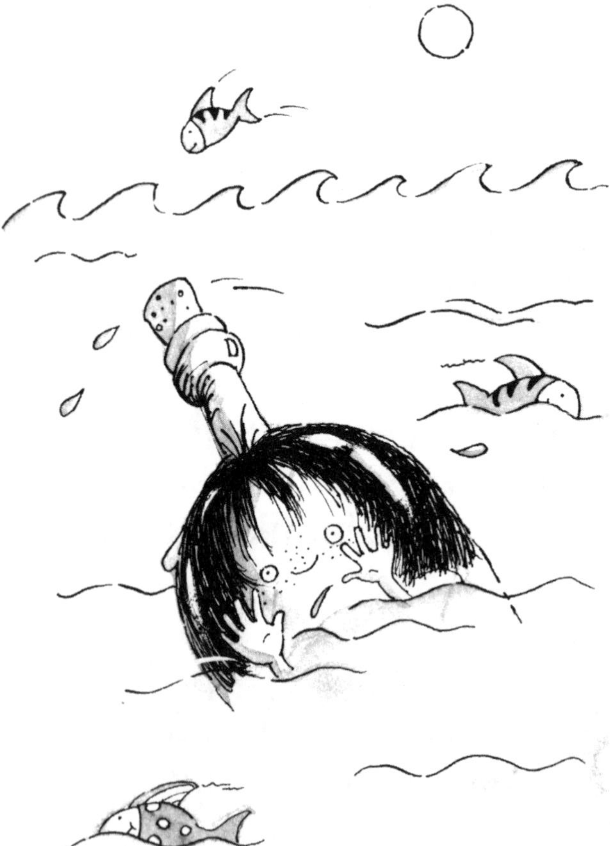

eyes are getting misty. Soon I will be a bottle filling up with salt water and sinking to the bottom of the ocean.

No, I won't! I'll try to float a little longer. I straighten up and lift my head.

Then do I get a shock! Past the sea of cars and traffic lights, I see the giant sign of the shopping mall where I often come with my family.

I feel as if I've received a jolt of energy. I start to run. Running, running toward my life-line.

8
At the mall

When I reach the mall I am out of breath and dripping like a doughnut that has just been dunked.

I take off my coat and sit down on a bench near the fountain. Just the sound of the water is enough to refresh me.

I recognize the rooster sign of the barbecue restaurant, the toyshop window full of toys, the merry-go-round where Angelbaby and Julian ride around on horses. I feel almost at home here.

What would be nice now is something to eat. It must be

getting late.

I look at my watch. With a little pang, I think of our granny clock at home. It's eleven o'clock.

ONLY ELEVEN O'CLOCK!

Even so I'm starving. My mother is right: you really should have something for breakfast. I open up my schoolbag.

The first thing I find is the bag of chips. I scoff them down like a real glutton.

Eleven o'clock is not the right time for a real meal or for a proper diet. Anyway, what's the point of running away from home if you're only going to do what you're supposed to do?

That's why I think I'll have chocolate-chip cookies for dessert. There, no sooner said

45

than done.

Yum-yum. These are good. I feel quite cheerful now.

I think I'll go to the toy store, without my parents, for once.

Wow, this is great! I can touch whatever I want. Games, books, cars, and even cartoon figures. They're all there: Snowy, Goofy, the Smurfs, Babar, even Mickey Mouse.

With a sharp pang, I think of my own Mickey, my night-light. The thought of him casts a shadow on all my fun.

Anyway, the saleslady is watching me. She seems to think it strange to see a kid in a toy-shop.

Honestly! I can't believe it! But I guess I'd better go.

I hurry out of the shop, and the

saleslady follows fast on my heels. She must think I stole something! I run away as fast as I can. My heart is racing. I don't stop until I'm far away, in front of a shop window filled with television sets.

I'm so frightened, I can't even tell what's on television. The police are sure to come and get me and take me away and put me in jail with the crooks.

I wish I could leave, but I can't seem to move. It's as if my feet are frozen in a block of ice.

All around me are crowds of people, like thousands of ants. I'm beginning to get dizzy. I can't tell where I am. The mall doesn't feel so much like home any more.

At home there are lots of

people too, but at least I know them all. And my parents do try to help.

Before my eyes fill with tears, I check my watch again. It's six o'clock.

SIX O'CLOCK!

That's impossible. That's TERRIBLE!

9
In the deep, dark woods

Like a maniac, I dash to the exit. Outside, it's already dark.

I almost fly down the road. I cross the street on a red light. A car swerves past me, honking furiously.

Two more traffic lights, and then I'm in the woods. I have to go through them to get back home.

The path narrows. It's much darker in here. The silence falls over me like a smothering blanket.

Suddenly a man looms up out of the darkness, with a huge dog.

"Never talk to strangers," my mother always warned me.

I walk past them. Then I hear footsteps behind me. It must be them. They're following me.

Right in front of my face I see a huge paw with long pointed claws.

PHEW! It was the shadow of a tree.

Will I never come to the edge of the woods? In the car it seems so short, but on foot it's more like a forest!

I feel sick to my stomach, and I'm shivering despite my many layers. I am sooooooo scared. I can't stand it!

"HELP! MUM! DAD! GRANNY!"

10
I can't believe it!

HELP! HELP! I'M...I'm in my bed!?! What! I'm in my bed!

I was dreaming. It was all only a dream.

WHEW!

To prove I really am home in my own bed, there's Mickey, shining brightly. My schoolbag is on the floor, flat as a pancake as usual.

Here comes Alexander. Now I know I'm home. I'm so happy, I just have to give him a kiss.

SMACK SMACK! Two big kisses. I just gave him two of the biggest kisses ever.

Alexander can't believe it. Do you know what he does? He runs out and tumbles down the stairs yelling, "Mum, Mum, Maddie is sick!"

He's right. I think I will stay home sick today. My tummy feels funny. And after such an action-packed nightmare, I need a little rest.

But dreams are a wonderful thing, don't you agree? They make you stop and think, anyway.

I think I will wait a little while before I really run away from home. Maybe a few years.

It's just too hard being a heroine all on your own. Much harder than being a big sister, that's for sure.

The First Novel series

Award-winning books for young readers — look for these and other titles in the series!

Arthur's Dad
by Ginette Anfouse

Arthur's dad is about to give up because he cannot find a babysitter for Arthur. He has had twenty three! But this time Arthur's dad thinks he has finally found a match for Arthur.

The Swank Prank
by Bertrand Gauthier

Hank and Frank Swank are twins. They look exactly alike, but they are not alike in any other way! Trying to be the smartest kids in school takes a lot of hard work and they have to learn to get along. Will they be able to do it?

Mooch and Me
by Gilles Gauthier

Carl and his best friend, Mooch, are nine. But, Mooch is a dog and that makes him sixty three! He is old, deaf, mostly blind, and gets Carl into loads of trouble. But Carl thinks he is the best dog that ever lived!

Look for these First Novels!

• *About Arthur*
Arthur Throws a Tantrum
Arthur's Dad
Arthur's Problem Puppy

• *About Fred*
Fred and the Flood
Fred and the Stinky Cheese
Fred's Dream Cat

• *About the Loonies*
Loonie Summer
The Loonies Arrive

• *About Maddie*
Maddie in Trouble
Maddie in Hospital
Maddie Goes to Paris
Maddie in Danger
Maddie in Goal
Maddie Wants Music
That's Enough Maddie!

• *About Mikey*
Mikey Mite's Best Present
Good For You, Mikey Mite!
Mikey Mite Goes to School
Mikey Mite's Big Problem

• *About Mooch*
Mooch Forever
Hang On, Mooch!
Mooch Gets Jealous
Mooch and Me

• *About the Swank Twins*
The Swank Prank
Swank Talk

• *About Max*
Max the Superhero

• *About Will*
Will and His World

Formac Publishing Company Limited
5502 Atlantic Street, Halifax, Nova Scotia B3H 1G4
Orders: 1-800-565-1975 Fax: (902) 425-0166